T0127618

NOTHING
FROM
NOTHING

# NOTHING
# FROM
# NOTHING

A Novella for None

* * * * * * * * * * * * * * * *

## N. NOSIRRAH

Illustrations by
### A. Nosirrah

SENTIENT PUBLICATIONS, LLC

First Sentient Publications edition 2009
Copyright © 2009 by N. Nosirrah

A paperback original

Cover design by Timm Bryson
Book design by Adam Schnitzmeier

---

Library of Congress Cataloging-in-Publication Data

Nosirrah, N. (Nevets)
  Nothing from nothing : a novella for none / N. NosirrAh : illustrations by A. Nosirrah.
       p. cm.
  ISBN 978-1-59181-088-9
  I. Title.
  PS3614.O7835N67 2009
  813'.6--dc22

                                        2009021323

Printed in the United States of America

10 9 8 7 6 5 4 3 2 1

SENTIENT PUBLICATIONS
A Limited Liability Company
1113 Spruce Street
Boulder, CO 80302
www.sentientpublications.com

# Contents

# Editor's Preface

* * * * *

IN FAIRNESS TO YOU THE READER, I MUST EXPLAIN that the following work is being published despite the protests of its author. Nosirrah is both a man of genius and, as often is the case with such creative energy, rather erratic.

Early on, Nosirrah entrusted me with the editing and publication of his literary work, a great honor for me and at the same time a life-long burden. He is not a man who would do well in the cutthroat environment of high-level, literary publishing. It is not just his odd appearance, his shrill and grating voice and tic-like mannerisms, nor his incessant attempts to seduce any and all of the female gender from secretary to executive. No, it is that for him to shift even a few moments from his creative expression would be to waste something rare and precious, and it is my sworn duty to protect him from all social and business pressures and to protect him from himself. I receive from him his words as they are, scrawled on napkins and scraps of paper, usually quite incoherent or illegible, and edit these rough stones into the jewels that you find so inspiring. I do only small work on his prose, adding punctuation and creating sentences and paragraphs by filling in nouns, adjectives, and other descriptive and connecting words.

Nosirrah does very well with verbs, but perhaps he is a bit obsessed with action and tends to exclusively use verbs with grunting sounds in between. He believes in *doing*, so he is following the direct instructions of his guru, Antisthenes, a philosopher who died in 365 BC—such is the time-bent world of Nosirrah.

As you might guess, since he has no sense of time, he also has no sense of story or structure, so I add this for the benefit of his reading public. While it may appear that I am more or less writing the entirety of his work, nothing could be further from the truth. He is the genius and I am just his loyal editor.

I am dedicated to this writer, this man, this wonder, but I will never see him again. I accept only his writing, never his presence, after what occurred between us in the torrid heat that was generated not just as a writer and editor, but as a man and a woman. He has written of it in *Chronic Eros*, and I will say nothing more other than that what he said was a pack of lies, but lies I was willing to overlook in order to let the remarkable book be published. For the record I have never owned a whip nor used it in the manner described, titillating as that may seem to a voyeuristic reader. I will admit to the hand-cuffs and latex outfits, but who doesn't own that sort of thing?

Nosirrah left me the material that was to become the book you now hold in your hands with a note saying that this book had taken him into non-existence and back, and he wondered if the world was ready for it. I edited this remarkable book and nearly lost my own mind in contemplating its message on the nature of nothing and the nothing that comes from nothing: that the everything we see is nothing, and the nothing we don't see is everything. I knew that this work must be published, that the world was not only ready for this work, but that it would transform us as never before. But Nosirrah began leaving me notes insisting that he get the manuscript back, that it should never be published, and that if it were ever published he would dedicate his life to tracking down every copy and destroying them all. He begged, he threatened, he even attempted to see me, and I was tempted to run to him once more, but I could not let him stop this book from changing the course of human consciousness.

Since you hold this book in your hands, you know that I have succeeded in its publication and Nosirrah has failed to suppress this book.

If, however, you hold this book and the world is not celebrating the publication of *Nothing from Nothing*, and you do not see this book in the hands of your friends, and on the cover of *Life* magazine, and being discussed by every television talk show host from Dick Cavett to Johnny Carson then you will know that I have published it but at the same time failed, and that Nosirrah has won in the end by destroying this miracle of words as he vowed he would do.

If this is so, then you hold perhaps one of the few, perhaps the only remaining copy, and it will be for you to take up the cause of bringing this book to the world. Read it, be transformed, and then you will know exactly what to do.

—*Lydia Smyth, Editor*

# Foreword

*　*　*　*　*

IT IS UNUSUAL TO FIND A FOREWORD WRITTEN to a novella, yet when Lydia Smyth asked me to write something to explain both this work of considerable mastery and its author, N. Nosirrah, whom I have known since childhood, I saw a chance to contribute something, however small, to this profound project.

Nosirrah is a chameleon, a man whose compassion and connection to the human condition and to the everyday people he encountered led him to a kind of fluidity of identification. He has no sense of time—by that I mean not time of day, but rather present, past or future, that is, where he stood in that continuum and whether he was flowing forward, backward, or in random temporal patterns—and this in combination with his flexible identity led him to inhabit many lives in many times as if these lives were his own. Perhaps those many lives were in fact his lives, after all these were not just the imaginings of a novelist, or as some say, a schizophrenic sociopath, but this is really trans-location of the mystic moving through the medium of divine madness, mind without boundary. He is convinced, for example, that he is the bastard child of Alice B. Toklas, the result of her one night stand with Franz Kafka in Berlin. It seems an impossibility—he seems hardly that old—yet nothing is impossible with Nosirrah.

Those of us who have the firm conviction of our selfhood, who are deeply attached to the elements of belief that give our lives meaning and who are certain that the past is known and behind us, the future ahead and unseen, will find the state of mind of Nosirrah quite difficult to comprehend. Yet despite this great challenge, we can easily see the brilliance of his words, the depth of his insight and the creative invention of his life in all of its cinematic detail.

For Nosirrah, life is a dream—not just a dream, but an agitated dream, interrupted by sudden gasping apneatic awakenings, then these awakenings themselves interrupted by dreams, until the whole of being is a dream that is awake—a state of awakening that has the richness and sinuous quality of hallucination, of delusion, but nevertheless a stark vision of reality itself deconstructed to its essential energy. Yes, he has been sent to psychiatrists more times than I can count, but he always came out of the seventy-two hour involuntary hold feeling that he had helped them and quite willing to return should life deliver him again to the psych ward.

Many have been taken aback by his relationship to women, and I myself have found it shocking to observe his animal magnetism in relation to women despite nature's unkind endowment of his truly repulsive physical characteristics, well noted in his writings. Here we must make a leap in our own consciousness to understand this is Nosirrah, a jnani who is beyond causality. Perhaps for you or me, a crude, anatomically descriptive pick-up line to a waitress during an otherwise sedate meal would be a shocking departure from social norms, but for Nosirrah, this is not just a buxom young woman, but the Goddess herself, and his attempts to seduce her, and the women in the booth behind him and the ones on the other side of the restaurant, and the policewoman called by the manager to eject him, are simply his worship of the Feminine Principal incarnate, his adoration of Shakti.

Equally disturbing is Nosirrah's fascination with urination and bodily secretions of all kinds, many of which seem to spontaneously erupt from him at inopportune times. This is not simply the infantile fixation of a man who was left to potty train himself and did so by reading a plumbing manual. When body liquids or semisolids squirt from Nosirrah these are the fluid stigmata of a saint, and the result of Nosirrah's Tantric mastery. In India and Nepal, Nosirrah, under the guidance of a Tantric master, performed long ritual meditations in that tradition so as to transcend the thoughts and feelings of disgust with all bodily fluids as well as other Hindu special concerns such as carrion, feces-eating dogs, and dead bodies, as well as clothes that have been in contact with a sick or dead body, food that has been spit upon, pecked at by birds, smelt at by cows, touched with the foot, sneezed on, or defiled by hair or insects and all other impure and polluted substances. In other words, when Nosirrah urinates, it is from his exalted perspective the release of nectar, and only for we who are still veiled in illusion does it appear to be stinky pee.

Dogs are of special interest to Nosirrah. In part this is due to his unusual upbringing in which there was virtually no acknowledgment of his existence. This led him to two profound but irreconcilable theories of self which he developed at a prodigiously young age. His first theory was that of the non-existence of a personal self in an intelligent and energetic non-dual universe. The second theory of self was that he was a dog.

Nosirrah would be well into his adolescence before he unified these two theories by developing cynophobia, the irrational fear of dogs, and hence an intense self-hatred of his delusional dog self as well as all the rest of the unfortunate canines living in his neighborhood. While his new phobia allowed him to meld his personality into a singular but depersonalized self, he would from that time on be morbidly interested in dogs biting and being bitten as you will see throughout this novella.

Who is Nosirrah and what is his message for mankind? I have been with him from nearly the beginning, and have listened to him as he traveled the world talking with those who needed to meet him, yet I can tell you only this: you, the reader, the seeker, the lover, the fool, are yourself the message that Nosirrah brings; you are the revelation and you are nothing, just as I am nothing, and Nosirrah is nothing, and from this nothing which we all are comes forth nothing, and this is the shattering, silent beauty expressed in this incomparable work written in precise and elegant words meant for none.

*—Nebirk Yallip*

# Preface

* * * * *

THOSE WHO UNDERSTAND THESE WRITINGS HAVE no need to meet me, those who do not understand have no reason to meet me, and those who need to meet me have no need to read my writings.

—N. Nosirrah

# 0

. . . . .

*Nothin' from nothin' leaves nothin'*
*You gotta have somethin'*
*If you wanna be with me*

— BILLY PRESTON

I FELL INTO AN ENDLESSLY DEEP HOLE.

You cannot hope to discover anything at all in this book.

Put this book down unless you cannot.

You cannot interpret these words, you can only read them.

You cannot read these words, you can only imagine that you are reading them.

You cannot imagine reading these words, you are being imagined.

Your imagination is not flexible enough to imagine itself.

Unless it is.

And then, it does not imagine, it only knows.

What it knows is that you are reading these words and interpreting them precisely.

What these words say is that they say nothing, that you say it all as you read them.

You find the meaning that is not there unless you construct it, and is still not there even if you construct it. Meaning is not there, it is constructed as there. There is nothing before it, there is nothing after it, there is nothing during it. There is no it. It is just a word, without meaning unless you construct that meaning, and then it has none, it just has construction.

You cannot understand that there is nothing that is something; you can only understand that there is something, or that there is nothing. *Either* is a universe that you understand. *Or* is a universe that you understand. This is dual and what is dual can be understood. If you want understanding then you must find another source, another book, another group of words. These words cannot bring you understanding, only chaos.

Some say chaos is freedom, but it is not. There is no freedom because there is no prison and no prisoner. Chaos doesn't bring you freedom, it brings you nothing, and takes away every-thing, then it takes away the nothing.

I will tell you nothing in this book and you will learn nothing from it. But this is the fail-ing of my logic. There is no one reading these words. They are not published. They will just be left on the paper—forms, symbols.

It is troubling, but it is true that this tome will become more and more difficult for you to follow as you progress through it. Better to turn your attention to something meaningful, impor-tant or at the least entertaining. If you continue, I cannot guarantee your safety, nor can I con-cern myself with your probable fragmentation and confusion as I am fully engaged in my own even as I write this. I struggle to move these fingers on this typewriter and to form coherence when incoherence is my true nature; you will struggle to form incoherence when coherence is your nature. My incoherence is far stronger than your coherence and you may wrestle this sentence to the ground of your knowing, but you are already tiring and I am just getting warmed up.

You cannot understand this but I will tell it anyway. I have looked into nothing. I have become nothing in that looking. But, this is not the extent of the emptying of my being. It is that I have looked *from* nothing. From that nowhere I have looked into a world which is full of form that does not know that form is nothing. I have seen you in that world, full of yourself, your troubles, your expectations, your loves, your fears. I have screamed at you to wake up, but, of course, you heard nothing. Yet, you could not have heard nothing, because that was the something I was screaming. You heard something; you heard your own mind filling in the wail of nothing with the sweet sound of yourself. I came back to you like a bodhisattva who swears to return life after life until all sentient beings are enlightened. But I am no bodhisattva and I care nothing for you or for enlightenment. I swore I would never come back to the world of form where there is nothing to save, nothing to give, and that nothing shatters all hope of redemption, all possibility of insight, all seeking for peace. Yet, I am back, writing this to you, and you cannot read it despite all your efforts. You can only construct the meaning of these words with the building blocks of what you already know, the fullness of your knowing, the something that you believe yourself to be. I came back because there is nowhere else. I am gesticulating to you who are as blind, deaf and dumb as a rock, a rock with the hubris that comes with the idea of self-awareness, but still a rock.

Nothing has been the bane of mankind and its silent helper. Nothing had to be discovered, invented, created. The Babylonians wrestled with it, the Greeks tried to ignore it, finally in India something of a zero emerged eight centuries before Christ. This was the zero of kha, nothingness, emptiness. The nothing of zero held the universe together, the googolplex of particles would collapse into a meaningless pile of integers without zeros to hold them in their places. Nothing holds the world together just as it holds mathematics together. The nothing

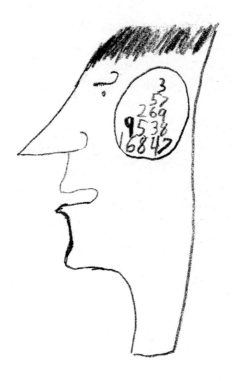

*The googolplex of particles would
collapse into a meaningless
pile of integers without zeros to
hold them in their places.*

of a zero is possibility where all other numbers are fixed somethings. Zero is more boundless than infinity, such is the creativity of nothing. And you cannot divide by using zero, consider that very deeply, you cannot divide anything by zero, not even zero by zero, it is impossible.

You are comfortable with your infinity of something, your endless flow of knowable experience, your center from which you look away from nothing. But all of your experience falls back into nothing, all your knowns become unknown, your center just a response of fear of the emptiness at your core. Even as you read these words you build your case for your own existence, finding meaning in this sentence, and forming an opinion of that meaning, and feeling the certainty of the opinion you have created of the meaning you have created of the sentence you have created. This house of cards of the self does not stand on anything firm, if it did it would fall down into a random pile, rather it floats in the space of nothingness where nothing holds it together, therefore nothing knocks it down. You misunderstand this cohesion for substance, for strength, for structure, and it is not any of these things. Your house of cards of self stands together as momentum, habit, inertia. Nothing allows this—empty space without friction, without counterforce, without resistance is what creates it. Nothing from nothing, the occurrence of no thing, of thingness that is nothing, is what destroys the illusion of self. Anything that touches the house of cards in the space of nothingness shatters it instantly. Nothing must touch you lest you be shattered. Nothing must touch you because it is already touching you. You are already shattered, your cards in a scattered pile that looks not at all like you, but like a house that is no longer a house and cards that are no longer cards. It is a magic trick of transformation. Nothing from nothing.

You can complain, you can cry, you can rant, you can scream, but nothing cares, nothing hears you, because there is no sound in a vacuum. You need something for your words to vibrate in, to crash into, to bounce off of, but if there is nothing there, then your words are nothing.

What first emerged from nothing in the beginning of the universe, the explosion of something from nothing, the event of creatio ex nihilo? What came from nothing, but nothing. Neutro-

*You can complain, you can cry, you can scream, but nothing cares.*

nium, just neutrons, not electrons or protons, not positive or negative, not yin or yang, but something which was nothing, nothing which was nothing, so neutral that the scientists of the twentieth century can only guess about it. Of course, suggested number on the periodic table is....zero. But they will find it someday, two, three, four, maybe more neutrons pushed together without anything else, an atomic structure so elemental as to be the very beginning point of matter from energy, form from formless. In the beginning there was the explosive creation of all that is and it was neutral, it was neutronium, it was zero. The physicists will find nothing in the form of neutrons, and they will be looking directly at the Godhead, which will burn them to a cinder. Like Captain Kirk heading into the center of the Doomsday Machine, the self must enter into the explosion of nothing. The Doomsday Machine's hull is made with what else but the impenetrable neutronium, no way to pierce it, no way to destroy it, no way to protect against it. Kirk must sacrifice his life to enter the very mouth of the Doomsday Machine. Of course, Kirk is contemporary television fiction, he is beamed away at the very moment of his demise, saved by a screenwriter whose job is to write this near death over and over in always new ways. What screenwriter will save you? What crew will beam you up in the final moments? Your self is crashing into the Doomsday Machine even now.

Star Trek is a sacred play, the scrolls of truth for this age, Kirk and Spock the paired opposites of the future, feeling and logic, truth and fiction. Truth and fiction are like parallel universes colliding or two sides of a coin run over by a trolley, or the buttered side of the toast and the other side, unless you like to butter both sides, which I do sometimes even though it does drip on your shirt when you try to eat it and that could be aggravating unless you don't change your shirt much and then who is going to notice since it is covered with beer stains, ketchup, sardine oil.

If you are following this text then you must know where I am going.

If you know where I am going then you know that I am going to Nothing.

I once visited Nothing, but you think I am joking. I found what I was looking for there. You might, too. You can go there yourself, although

I don't recommend it. It exists and it doesn't exist at the same time, it is a place called Nothing, Arizona. Mile Post 148 1/2, Highway 93, Population 4, more or less. But if you go there and there is nothing, it is because you are looking for something, and you won't find it there, you will just find your endless looking. Go there looking for nothing and you will find Nothing, and it will be exactly what you are looking for, just as it is, just as you are, just nothing. You may still think I am joking but I never visited Nothing nor will you ever visit there either. Send me a postcard when you get there, they sold them at the gas station when I was there last. I will tell that tale another time, in another way, the story of my life, the story of no life, the life I will write about in the future about my past which will always and forever be read in the present. It is my semi-autobiographical novella and I call it *Practical Obsession*, for life is exactly that, isn't it?

I was a fool then, and a wanderer, just like the Tarot card, The Fool with a dog nipping at me, walking along the edge of a cliff. Is it faith that allows us to walk on the edge of destruction in our lives, or is it naiveté? The Fool is

*I was a wanderer, the Fool with
a dog nipping at me.*

oblivious to these categories, each step is its own adventure, its own moment, its own universe with only the dog of time, the hounding of reality taking a bite out of his Foolish ass here and there. And, of course, in the Tarot cards, The Fool is number 0, he is nothing and doesn't seem to even notice.

Nothing is a noun, a pronoun, an adverb and an adjective. It is not a verb. Only God is a verb, just like Bucky Fuller says. But he goes on, Bucky that is, not God, although sometimes when I listen to Bucky it is hard to know the difference, but Bucky goes on to say, "Yes, God is a verb, the most active, connoting the vast harmonic reordering of the universe from unleashed chaos of energy."

You can disregard everything that has been written up until now; it is there just to throw off any casual reader, anyone who thought they would pick up a book out of curiosity, or worse, out of interest. What has come before this is a smoke screen of verbiage designed to eliminate most readers so that only the few would get to the potent essence of this book. You are approaching it now, so beware. It is not for the faint hearted nor for the arrogant. Indeed

this was written while I was under the influ-
ence of a hypnotic trance induced by a woman
so seductive that even her complete rebuke of
my passionate interest, including a restraining
order and a newly acquired attack dog, could
not shake me of the compelling belief that my
destiny held more than nothing, yet far less
than something. I could not have her (and dear
Lydia as my editor and muse you must forgive
me my attractions to other women but I am
a man, no, not just a man, but I am Nosirrah
and *Nosirrah is Man*, but let me get back to
the narrative before you edit this out), but the
desire arising in my loins, which could find no
expression in the world of flesh, drove me into
a kind of energetic spiritual mania that has destroyed everything and at the same time created
something from that destruction. What follows
is that something and there is now no way back
to the innocence of a sweet nothing.

Here I should put some kind of disclaimer,
a warning. But how shall I warn you of something which is nothing? It is something like a
landslide and you only have a moment to get
out.

Here are the warning signs of a landslide; if

you notice one or more of these then get out now:

Changes occur in your landscape, such as patterns of storm-water drainage on slopes, land movement, small slides, flows, or progressively leaning trees.

Doors or windows jam for the first time and cracks appear in plaster, tile, brick, or foundations.

Outside walls, walks, or stairs begin pulling away from the building and widening cracks appear on the ground, streets or driveways. Underground utility lines break, water breaks through the ground surface in new locations, fences, retaining walls, utility poles, or trees tilt or move. A faint rumbling sound that gets louder as the landslide nears. The ground may begin shifting under your feet. Unusual sounds, such as trees cracking or boulders crashing together, might indicate moving debris.

To continue with this book is to fail to heed these warnings. Get out now. Cracks are forming in the earth as it shifts beneath your feet. Transformation comes with as much devastation and with less warning. So get out.

Continue at your own risk.

*Continue at your own risk.*

Caveat emptor.

If NORAD tracked this book, it would order it shot down.

The Surgeon General Warning: Reading further can cause immediate loss of identity.

Abandon all hope, ye who enter here—Bridge Out.

But, if you are still reading, then read on. And good luck.

When I was enlightened, the world was very clear. It was a world that was one, that flowed to and fro without edges or containers other than the borders that maya liked to create. It was an idyllic place, no, not a place, but a quality, a formless energy that was both me and not me at the same time. I had function if not form in that enlightenment, I could help and heal, I could love without condition, I could translate from the one to the many in lyric terms, a musica universalis in which all elements of the vast everything connected in balance, harmony and beauty.

I miss my enlightenment. It left me, just as easily as it came, a beautiful love whose capriciousness leaves me embittered but still craving one more chance. It left my heart broken, my ears deaf to the music, my tongue rough and sharp. The energy that once flowed upward into infinite space, now pressed down, compressing me into even less than myself, weighted by a heaviness that was far more than the opposite of what had once been light. You might say that I am back to where I began, but where I began was simply contraction and illusion; where I am is contraction without the illusion and that is something of an entirely different order. A something that is nothing, a nothing from nothing.

A call to God will go unanswered; there is no one to call and no one to answer. No understanding is left, no purpose is left, no diversion is left. This is nothing, it is not Heaven and it is not Hell, it is a Purgatory without qualities, a liminal state without transformation, a Bardo without rebirth.

This is not Sartre's nothingness that is subsequent to being, or Hegel's nothingness that is opposite of being. This is being nothingness. The philosophers may write about nothingness looking back at it, from an ascending position, happy to report on something that they no longer can touch, or they may write from their mired depression, sunk so far into the quality that they want only to escape by the thin rope of narrative. But, none write from being nothingness. Of course, why would they write? Why would I write? I do, but I know that I write nothing from nothing, that I have no more control over the meaning of what is written than you do who read it and think that you do not understand it, or far worse, are sure that you do.

I have been advised to seek help with this. Clinicians are sure that this is depression and list the symptoms as if they are reading my mind. They list loss of interest in activities; no emotional expression but feeling sad, anxious, hopeless; worthlessness; social withdrawal; being slowed down; sleep disturbance; trouble concentrating, remembering, or making decisions; unusual restlessness or irritability; headaches; digestive disorders; and thoughts of death. That is the mind of Nosirrah, without a doubt, a cesspool of dysfunction and detritus of a life of a spiritual vagabond, but that is not nothing.

All of mind, all of my mind, all of your mind, is this depression. It lives in anxiety and it lives from anxiety. Its deepest fear is death, and it dwells on the fear so thoroughly that it cannot find relationship, it cannot concentrate, it cannot remember anything else, it cannot rest. If this mind is all that I am, then I would agree to this diagnosis, and undergo the shock therapy that is so in vogue now, and wake up foggy, but free from any thoughts that will torment me. If this mind is all that I am, then I could take the tranquilizers that the doctors love to give so that even though my thoughts continue to describe their emotionless irritations, I will not care at all, I will be oh, so happy.

But there is more than thought, so much more than thought. There is nothing. It does not care about death or the thoughts that fear death or Nosirrah or you. In that nothing there is not depression or elation either one, there is not even the flat affect of emotionlessness. There is nothing and nothing has no affect.

Shall we modify this nothing to make it better? Go ahead. Give it your best therapy; they thought once that Skinner could do something for me. You may think that Skinner only worked on rats and monkeys, but the truth is far darker. They put Nosirrah in an operant conditioning chamber and started rewarding for normal, happy thoughts. Nosirrah came out of the experiment

a few weeks later a happy man, no, an enlightened man. He saw that thought was attracted
to the notion of existence, and that happiness
was the expression of that magnetism. Green
light, reward. Existence took place in the moment as the movement of thought that was
generated simply by the resistance to the nothingness. Green light, reward. Nothingness ex-
truded thought into existence as happiness and
if nothingness did not do this, there would be
nothing, no thing and then a small but extreme-
ly painful electric current would jolt nothingness
into action. Red light, pain. Operant conditioning, the avoidance of pain, the attraction of
pleasure. Green light on. Food pellet drops. Red
light on. Electric current shocks. Scholarly types
in white lab coats looking intently, taking notes.
Happiness results from following the green light
and avoiding the red light. Nosirrah was happy
when he wasn't being shocked; Nosirrah was
not being shocked so he was happy. In only a
few weeks, Nosirrah was cured of his melan-
choly. A success story. But not in the way you
might think. It was success in Nosirrah's terms,
not in Skinner's. I saw I was happy, but I also
saw I was conditioned to be happy, and that

made me very sad. I also saw that the nothing that was shocked into thought wasn't nothing, it was a something—avoidance. Nothing was beyond pleasure and pain. I stopped avoiding the shock and wanting the pleasure and the shock became pleasurable and the pleasurable became shocking. I also went a little manic, tore up the laboratory, managed to connect one of the lab assistants to the electric current and utilized my recent urine sample as a fragrant anointment of the walls and floors. I felt pain and pleasure in doing so, but I didn't express either one since I was now unashamedly depressed and my affect had returned to flat.

I still have a hard time driving because of the red lights, I have to look away or I experience deep electrical currents throughout my body and I become lost in the pleasure of it and through that doorway I am not lost but I am found, I was blind but now I see that I am nothing. I don't drive often because I have the feeling one day I will run over someone at a red light, and I pray that God will intervene, but I would be surprised if he bothers to.

What would God care about this nothing? *Ex nihilo nihil fit.* Nothing comes from nothing...

not even God. I will have to take this up with God if I ever find him. Maybe God doesn't care, but the theologians do. In the face of nothing they scream *Creatio Ex Nihilo*. It is not nothing from nothing, it is creation from nothing, by God.

Some may ask if this God is so powerful as to exist even in nothingness and to create a universe from nothing, then why did he not also create a set of clear instructions? Why did he allow evil? Why is there no evidence that we came from nothing? But all of these questions are predicated on *creatio ex nihilo*, when all we have to do is to turn to *ex nihilo nihil fit* to answer everything by reducing our questions and ourselves to dust and that dust to atoms and those atoms to the electric fields of subatomic particles enveloping only space and nothing more.

Can creation out of nothing take place without God? Vacuums do not suck things, they just create space into which things are pushed. Vacuums are not doers, the doing happens without the vacuum's effort or energy. Vacuum, then something. Nothing then creation. Then nothing. Like twinkling stars, on then off. Nihilo.

Creatio. Nihilo. But this is not the thing itself, this is the ground and the groundless out of which the energy of life sparks. What there is in nothing is energy, not expressed, just potential. Nothing is energy, it is life, it is everything. Vacuum energy is what Mr. Wizard and the other science guys call it, and when they start to calculate the power of nothing it is off the scale, they have to renormalize it, take the infinite back to something they can relate to. If they didn't do that, then it would look like there was an unlimited energy contained in nothing that could be tapped for an endless supply of free energy. Tesla called it radiant energy, Nosirrah calls it God.

You may find energy flowing from these words, but there is infinitely more energy flowing from the space between these words, the very space between these very words. Yet you can not imagine, or think about, or use nothing. It is unavailable to your thinking mind, your planning, your grasping. All that you seek, all that you want, all that you dream lies in nothing, but you look for it in something. You are attracted to the formless but you settle for form. You crave the infinite but you accept the limited.

You starve for love but you eat the scraps of social arrangements and wonder why you still hunger.

God is nothing, and from nothing, and you cannot see him, only your shallow beliefs. As a something you are blocked at every turn, as nothing you can pass through walls as if nothing was in your way. You are so much more nothing than you are something, so much more space than object, more dream than real.

In that dream I am in Berlin again, it is 1933 and I am walking on Linden to the Berlin State Opera House, the Staatsoper unter den Linden when Erich Kleiber was still its heart and soul. I did not know this of course because I was just nine years old. I did not know that Kleiber would leave the Berlin Opera rather than agree to forgo the music of Jewish composers, declared degenerate by the Nazis. I did not know that he would return after a world war, only to resign again without so much as lifting his baton, rather than submit to the Communists who now controlled the Opera.

As I walked along in my innocence, I did not know that books were burning in the streets of Berlin or that the Reichstag was aflame, I was too young. But, I knew that nothing came from nothing, that even with the roaring energy of the time, the hate, the fear, that nothing would come from it in the end but the rubble of the Opera House, bombed into submission along with the German nation. I knew then what I could see and hear, the sounds from the Berlin Opera House, in 1933, of a symphony in D minor, though I didn't know its name, or that Bruckner was its composer, or that Fritz Zaun was conducting. I only knew that as a boy I was touched to the core of my being by the sounds of this nothing symphony, a symphony numbered 0, Bruckner's *Symphony No. 0 in D minor*, music that was nothing and everything, and that Bruckner himself didn't know what he could do with it, or even if it should be, or where it even came from.

But that 0 penetrated deeply into this boy holding that hand of a woman who held the hand of nothing. Gertrude Stein might be famous for the rose that was a rose that was a rose, but the boy was a nothing was a nothing even as her pudgy, clammy hand clenched mine, Alice walking three steps behind, Daddy Kafka nowhere to be found, never to be mentioned, fading into nothing himself, the nothing from which came this nothing called Nosirrah.

Did Fritz Zaun make it through the war? He wasn't a Jew it doesn't seem, so he kept working in Berlin. I have never found out what became of the man who extracted something from Bruckner's nothing and delivered it to me where I carry it still. He must have survived part of the war because Ulvi Erkin told me Zaun conducted Erkin's piano concerto late in 1943 in Berlin. The German 6$^{th}$ Army had surrendered in Stalingrad just months before and the Allies had burned Hamburg to the ground. Then the bombing of Berlin intensified and the Opera House was bombed into nothing. Where was Zaun? Under the rubble, his baton clenched in his hand? Escaped to the countryside awaiting the Russians? Taken up a rifle with the other old men and boys to fight for the Fatherland? Why did he stay? Maybe he was too old to do anything but conduct the music even as the bombs fell, maybe he felt that the music would protect him as it always had, maybe he saw nothing so clearly that all of the war, all of the pain, all of the destruction passed through him and transformed into the sounds of a new symphony heard even now when we listen from that space of emptiness.

Now that I am old like Zaun I suppose that bombs would not bother me as much as they did when I was young. Then I imagined that there was a life I could lose, that there was a missing future that would not be and a past that could never be looked back upon. I did not die from a bomb, by then I was safely tucked away at 27 rue de Fleurus in Paris and later the country house in Bilignin and did not suffer like that. But how was it that I survived unscathed since Gertrude Stein was a Jew and a lesbian, I was her son, well, Alice's son, but Alice was a Jew, too, so, wasn't I a Jew? I think Uncle Bernie—Bernard Fay to you—must have protected us. But though protected from the bombs, still I did not survive because to Alice Toklas and Gertrude Stein I was not seen, I was not heard, I did not exist. They had each other; they had no need of me and all that I reminded them of, Alice's indiscretion, Gertrude's jealousy, and with Kafka as the lover, of all people. I was the son begat by a cockroach, and so I could only come out when the lights were off; during the day I could only be nothing.

What life I had I have lost by living, there is only a little future left and the past is empty except for questions like, "What happened to Fritz Zaun?" But, I know the answer, what happened to Fritz Zaun has happened to me and it is happening to you. We all lie in the rubble of our life and hear the music of the universe, the music of nothing at all, and we dream that we live again in Berlin, live again in a time and a place where we never lived to begin with.

That is all a dream, one I choose not to dwell on; rather I would like to dream the dream of the blond haired beauty on horse back, my love, my delight, my heart, my eros, whom I meet in the forest where the paths come together, eyes meeting, but the paths diverge and the forest swallows her up again. I could dream that dream a million times over and over because in that meeting I am seen so deeply that I am the seer, I am both as one, I am neither, I am nothing and it is all beauty, just beauty.

But I am awake, not dreaming and I am Nosirrah, obsessed with people and worlds that I remember but never actually encountered, and even more obsessed with people and worlds that I encountered but cannot remember. There is an entanglement of reality in my being in which the Akashic records have merged with my psychic structure and I am all things and all times and all conditions in potential, and any thing at any time under some condition in any moment. My life stretches over more years than my age would suggest or my body would show. Was I nine years old in 1933, or was it 1943, or 1953 or 1963?

John Kennedy was alive in 1960, and so I must have been a child then because didn't I meet him in Brookhaven, Pennsylvania, met him only in the most cursory of ways, he in an open topped white convertible in a motorcade that could only exist because there had not been an assassination yet in an open topped convertible. He reached over to take the hand of a young man who looked at him with hope, that was me and it was 1960 not 1963, but his eyes were not on me as he took my hand, his eyes were on the young woman some few feet behind me, a beautiful blond woman, whose eyes were not on Kennedy, but on me. I told him not to let go, not to look at her, that I could change history by bending time, that he and I could go to 1964, and he could go for a second term, and no one would even notice. But he couldn't take his eyes off her, he let go of my hand and the motorcade rolled slowly on from Brookhaven directly to Dallas, three years in a moment, to death and a light so bright that even the blond hair of the beautiful woman paled next to it. And at that moment, in 1963 and in 1960, a moment in both times, the beautiful blond woman and I were melded into one.

I went looking for the blond woman in all the wrong places and in all the wrong ways and in *Chronic Eros* I tell this tale of ecstatic agony, but in that pursuit I stumbled into a spiritual seminar, there were so many in those days, the psychedelic Sixties, and if you didn't find enlightenment you would certainly find some blissful ladies and that for Nosirrah is a religious experience. Om Shanti Shanti.

The teachers were called gurus then because gurus didn't have a bad name yet, Maharshi was chasing Mia Farrow but no one knew it, so anyone who had been to India or even knew someone who had been to India or who had done a weekend with one of the Japanese guys coming over to create Zen as a new brand of affectation, was suddenly a guru and could pick up girls without much effort. I wanted in, so I went for my weekend, figuring I would come out as a guru.

The teacher's name was Peter Kornstein, from a non-practicing New York Jewish upper middle class family, dropped out of law school, hit the spiritual seminar circuit, took the name Hari Deep Diss and practiced looking serene every day. Except he didn't like my sunflower seeds; in those days I was experimenting with the Sacred Sunflower Seed Diet I had read about in the *East West Journal*, it was a macroeconomic diet with perfectly balanced yin out the yang, which meant shelling and eating sunflower seeds pretty much all the time, shelling them with my teeth (which I still had at that point, or at least many of them) and then spitting out the shells and swallowing the kernel. As you might imagine this did not go well with the quiet lecture on the spirit of nothingness. It didn't really work as a diet either, unless you are a squirrel. Nevertheless despite the interruption of the teacher's profundity, I did manage to shell, spit and swallow a large part of a three pound bag of sunflower seeds during the course of a rather lengthy lecture and meditation. Well, actually I

*The Sacred Sunflower Seed Diet—it is sacred eating and sacred spitting.*

wasn't there for the whole event because they did throw me out about halfway through, maybe because I was pretty inaccurate with the spitting and kept hitting the people in the row in front of me with the shells and occasionally landing just plain spittle sans shell.

But the spiritual talk by Hari Deep Diss was on the nature of emptiness, which is apropos to the subject of this book, so I shall recount it here, it went something like this:

Deep Diss was droning on, "In the *Tao De Ching* it is written:

> Thirty spokes connect to the wheel's hub;
> It is the hole in the middle that makes it useful.
> Shape clay into a container;
> It is the space inside that makes it useful...
> Usefulness comes from what is not there."

There were murmurs and slight gasps as the attendees took in the depth of this. The front row of lovely ladies nearly swooned, possibly considering what it might be like to have their clay shaped by Deep Diss.

Deep Diss went on, "Standing still in the midst of the chaos, moving despite the stagnation of our habits, being is the full embrace of the useless and the useful, the dreams and the failures, the fullness and emptiness. Being is simple presence, neither concerned with liking or the disliking, but only just here, just now, just being.

The redwood tree stands in its place for two thousand years. The winter comes and goes, the summer comes and goes. Birth and death occurs all around. The redwood tree stands in its place."

I had an urgent question for Peter a.k.a. Deep Diss, so I raised my hand, not being sure whether to just interrupt. He seemed to look right through me, and I didn't know if that was because he was looking at my energy field, he was very nearsighted or he was trying to ignore me. I waved harder. He ignored. I waved hard and cleared by throat. He ignored harder. I waved, cleared phlegm and called his name.

"...The wind whistles through the branches, the birds twitter and call from its limbs, the squirrels gather its cones scampering here and there. The redwood tree is silent, it stands in its place." Deep Diss tried to go on.

Waving, clearing, calling and spitting, I would not be denied. If I am honest with myself, I don't like to be ignored, but I don't particularly like this character flaw, so I try to ignore it. Finally, Deep Diss stopped his talk, and said, sounding, it seemed to me, a bit more irritated than an enlightened man should, "Yes, what is it?"

"Deep Diss, oh wise master, where is the rest room?" He seemed stunned by my question, which I thought rather basic, making me begin to question his mastery.

"Sir, it is out the door, to your left and down the hall."

"Deep Diss, your honor, I tend to get lost, is it on the right or the left when I go down the hall?" I have never had an easy time with directions, I try to listen carefully, but I tend to fall into the spaces between words, and then begin to fear that I will fall into the spaces between tiles on the floor, then I start screaming, which usually makes me forget the fear, but also makes me forget the directions. It is better if someone just takes me where I need to go.

"Sir, I am giving a public lecture here, I cannot give you endless detail on the bathroom. And will you stop spitting those shells around the room; this is a spiritual space, a place of reflection and meditation." A hundred blissed out followers nodded in agreement.

"Deep Diss, your highness, I am truly sorry, I am just a worm of a man, and I crawl before your magnificence but to find true emptiness I have to vacate my you know what, my number 1, you know what I mean. And, I am on the Sacred Sunflower Seed Diet recommended by Michio Kushi and therefore must continuously eat and spit, but it is sacred eating and sacred spitting. Would you like a handful? They're organic."

Deep Diss was losing his glow and was leaning forward towards me, his eyes now bugging out just a little too much for my comfort. I explained that I was also spatially dyslexic, going left when I should go right, once even failing in a suicide attempt when I threw myself behind a bus. I truly needed help with the bathroom and pretty much immediately.

His followers were beginning to talk amongst

themselves, and I could only guess that they were considering overpowering me and taking my sacred, organic sunflower seeds. Admittedly, I might have overreacted by jumping to my feet and taking a defensive stance utilizing my prior Okinawan karate training, and at the same time spilling my seed. I also dropped my sunflower kernels all over the place, it was really a mess, my seed and my seeds everywhere. I do that when I get overexcited, the seed part that is, and there were some very cute yoginis in the room, especially that one in the row in front of me with the red hair and the flimsy peasant blouse, now flecked with sunflower seed shells and saliva, of course. But, I think she might have been attracted to me.

Deep Diss jumped out of his repose, face red, and shrieked, "I don't give a rat's ass about your goddamned sunflower diet or your over-filled bladder, get your pocked-marked ass out of here."

You might wonder how he knew about my scarred butt, but no, we had not been intimate although I am sure he wanted that, rather I was at that very moment mooning him. That pretty much did it for the crowd, they all moved in to remove me from the room, and I must say that for a bunch of skinny, spiritual vegetarians, in the end they did know how to scratch and bite pretty well, or they were quick learners watching me defend myself, as scratching and biting has always been my specialty, since truth be told I never got very far in my Okinawan karate training.

I was finally evicted from the place, and was left with no viable option but to urinate on their front door, next to the sign that said, "Friday Meditation: Come Here for Peace." As I reread it, I realized my error, I thought it said, "for a Piece."

I heard that Deep Diss gave up his spiritual teaching career after that night and moved to Chicago to start a chain of pizza parlors. This was the sixties, there was so much magic in the air, you could be a guru one moment and then start a business the next, or if you were really good you could roll it into one and do a lot of business as a guru.

The only alternative in those days was to become a radical political type. It was not really that groovy to work for the election of your local congressman, it was somewhat hip to work for a national candidate, although it became obvious that anyone even remotely honest would be assassinated. So politics took to the streets, which meant organizing, leafleting, marching and hanging with girls you could radicalize enough to get them into bed. This became a problem when the girls actually did get radicalized and didn't like being called girls, and kicked your sorry butt out on the street. That was the real meaning of taking politics to the streets, which in my case meant not only being thrown out of the communal residence by feminists who took exception to my leering comments, my off color jokes and a libido generally gone hyper, and come on lines like, "You have come a long way, baby, and I'd walk a mile in Marlboro Country for a lucky strike with you, that would mean fine taste that is good like it should or I will eat my hat, so Lady be Kool, because Nosirrah tastes better, tastes fresher, too." I was riffing and jamming Madison Avenue's cigarette selling into a sales pitch about me to the women in the household because if it works to sell chopped up weeds in rolled up paper that you burn while it creates cancerous tumors in you then it might get me close to an attractive woman despite my chronic gum disease, occasional psoriasis flare-ups and striking nostril hair. But I never had a chance to find out if cigarette slogans that were pounded into the mind of each of us could be ridden all the way into the recesses of a woman's bed, because I was permanently removed from the neighborhood under threat of physical harm when I began picketing the house demanding equal rights for what was termed "male chauvinist pigs" in the quaint vernacular that has developed in the last decade. Now I have never been too certain about my gender identity, and I don't care that much for pork, but I am proud to be aligned with Nicolas Chauvin from whence the word chauvinist is derived.

Chauvin you may recall was a fanatic follower of Napoleon, wounded seventeen times in battle, severely maimed really, and loyal to the end even when the French nation had turned against the emperor and mocked all that Napoleon stood for, all five feet two inches of him. Chauvin stood by and no doubt above his Emperor even when Napoleon lost the battle of Waterloo, and Napoleon lost mainly because he had hemorrhoids and couldn't sit on his horse for long periods of time and hence couldn't see

*Nicholas Chauvin - wounded seventeen
times and loyal to the end*

the battlefield and even though this is a novel
and you may wonder about what is true and
what is not true, it is a fact agreed upon by
historians that Napoleon was short with hemorrhoids, couldn't sit on his horse, so couldn't see
the battlefield, and so lost the war and this is
as fundamentally true as that Richard Milhous
Nixon is in the White House, in other words,
we cannot tell fact from fiction, truth and fan-
cy merge into a nightmare world that we must
navigate without any real ultimate knowledge
of whether it is the disturbing fantasy of my
broken mind that I am traversing or some objective but truly odd universe, and in the case of
Nixon I would like to believe that this is simply
a dark recess of traumatized psyche that could
be altered by meditation, psychedelics or free
love into a different reality, but in the case of
Napoleon's hemorrhoids changing history I like
to believe that it is absolutely true because I
read it somewhere and as a result I do like to
add bran to my diet and by doing so I feel that
I am altering history. Sometimes I feel that way
about prune juice too, but not always.

If hemorrhoids are history then bowel health
is the ultimate power to change it. Contemplate

that every day when you are sitting on your porcelain throne.

But back to Nicholas Chauvin for a moment, I feel a deep resonance with him because he was like I am, he was an obsessive personality, mocked by his entire country for his unpopular beliefs and disfigured to the point of revulsion. I am a Chauvinist, and as such I have an unreasoning, overenthusiastic and aggressive allegiance to my own beliefs. Male Chauvinist is redundant. Chauvinist pig is demeaning to the porcine species. Just Chauvinist will do. Call me that and I will thank you for you have called me what I am, you have seen me thoroughly.

But while you are at it, call yourself what you are. You are a Chauvinist, with a fanatic allegiance to your beliefs. You believe in your beliefs, but you don't call them beliefs, you call them truths. You gather with others like you for protection, you glare at those not like you, who don't know the truth. You won't admit your Chauvinism, or if you do you won't call it that, you will call it love of your country, faith in your religion, commitment to your marriage, loyalty to your company. You are a patriot, a parishioner, a spouse, a parent, an employee, but you are an extremist believer, a militant who holds together your life by uncompromising loyalty to the superiority of what you know, what you have and what you are. That is Chauvinism and welcome to the club.

Maybe you have heard the famous saying, "History is a set of lies that people have agreed upon." You might find it amusing that this was a statement by Napoleon, according to historians. Or was it? What are your lies that you make into your history? What is the truth you don't dare remember? And by the way, Napoleon wasn't 5 feet, two inches tall, that is a lie of history that we all know to be true, his height, measured in the French feet and misstated into our measurements, was actually nearly 5' 7" which in his day was tall. Or was he? Chauvin didn't care, for him Napoleon was truth, there was nothing else.

Chauvin and I are so alike that we are like one: fanatic, reviled, repulsive. I embrace what I am and in that there is something from nothing, one without an opposite, without an explanation, without an excuse, just one.

Sunyata, nothingness, emptiness, nirvana, mu, bodhi, soku hi, zero, empty set, vacuum, null, no-operation.

Nothing is better than this.

Except one thing. And that is One is better than None. That is why there is something in the universe and not nothing. Something from nothing. One thing from nothing.

I

* * * * *

*The First is that whose being is simply in it-
self, not referring to anything nor lying behind
anything.*

—CHARLES SANDERS PEIRCE

I FELL INTO AN ENDLESSLY DEEP WHOLE.

First, about first grade.

I had an old school teacher in elementary
school who saw things in blackboard and white.
She had been teaching for a thousand years in
the same room with the same first graders, just

different names and faces.

I was not much for school but even then I had a fascination with nothing and with the fundamental unity, or one.

On a fine autumn day she asked me, "If you had a dollar and you asked your friend Nebirk to give you another dollar, how many dollars would you have?"

"One,' I answered.

"You don't know your arithmetic," she said.

And I replied, "You don't know Nebirk."

Nebirk told me that as a joke, so I wrote it into this book because I thought it was funny. It seemed funny when I heard it from Nebirk, but it doesn't seem so funny now.

Of course my elementary school teacher didn't know anything about none or one either, only about being in that room scaring the hell out of six year olds, which she did very well, by the way. Without my imaginary friend Nebirk, I would have gone crazy in those early school years, although later he claimed that he had imagined me and things got a little confusing for a few years while Nebirk and I sorted out exactly what was going on.

Teachers are significant, icons, archetypes, they confer their knowledge, they withhold conferring their credential. No first grader simply announces that he is done and moving on to second grade, or more radical, is moving on to life. There is too much fear of the unknown, too much indoctrination that the teacher holds something that I do not, and if I just wait, and play along, I will get it, I will have it, I will be safe. Passing on to second grade is safety for a first grader. What is safety for you? Are you looking for a teacher to tell you it is all right to move on?

Strange is the life that does not accept any teacher, or is too honest about who is a teacher and who is not. Even Bruckner had to face this, and it almost destroyed him, and perhaps this is what took him to the depths of nothing. Who would you align yourself with, Wagner or Brahms? Back Brahms and you are a made man, the talk of Vienna, renowned for your talent and genius. Back Wagner and you are no longer welcome, reviled, outcast. Old School never wants New School. *What is this rubbish with Bakunin and Schopenhauer, this Wagner is a madman, and so must be Bruckner.* But Bruckner loved

Wagner's work and paid the price of his love, love always has a price, not just at the point of purchase, but forever and a day.

And why do I love Bruckner? A visionary, unknown, despised, misunderstood, unrecognized until he was too old to care, Bruckner is a God to Nosirrah, he is the soul of Nosirrah, Bruckner *is* Nosirrah. Yet, I don't listen to his music, Bruckner is not a teacher to me, nor was Wagner a teacher to him. There is no authentic claim on the connection to the stream of consciousness, I can no more claim Bruckner, than he can claim Wagner, than you can claim Nosirrah. We each construct from that common stream, with no one to attribute, and no one to blame. Beware the claims of the student more so even than the claims of the teacher. Beware the claims of the spiritual seeker more so even than the claims of the guru.

As a matter of fact, I was told once that Wagner was walking on a street in Dresden one day and came across a rather mediocre violinist who was playing the overture from *Tristan und Isolde.*

Wagner could hardly stand it and chastised the musician, "You are playing this much too slowly!" before storming off.

The violinist, recognizing the famous composer *enfant terrible* called after him, "Thank you, Herr Wagner, danke, danke schoen!"

The next day, Wagner was walking down the same street and there was the violinist, playing the same piece and this time at the right tempo. Behind the violinist was a new sign, "Student of Richard Wagner."

I know that this is a true story, even though it is also an old joke, because I was there, it was Nosirrah playing the violin, or so I remember it. I wouldn't have chosen Wagner over Brahms, not because of the politics of the Viennese music scene, but because Wagner was a teacher, he tried to instruct the world on how to live, not just instruct but to command the world how to live. Brahms was a romantic, he believed in love and he was Schumann's protégé. Schumann once wrote a piece with the beginning notation "Play as fast as possible," then later in the piece wrote, "Faster." Schumann saw that there was no instruction, there was no teacher, there was no student, there was just energy without limitation taking you where you did not want to go. As fast as possible. Now faster.

I love Schumann, Bruckner and yes, even Wagner, but I only listen to rock and roll. I am just following Schumann's lead. Faster. Faster. If I could just play those rock chords faster and faster, then you would see the bodies fly around, dancers in a frenzy charging the stage and throwing themselves off, back into the audience, writhing and screaming, drunk and puking, punk kids on an energy bender. That's what I will call it, Puke Rock, or something like that, those pissed-off punk kids will like that name, a new movement that is theirs, but it will have to wait until the rock and roll of this decade degenerates into middle aged smugness. But when the rockers sell out, Nosirrah will pick up the microphone and scream in rage, and pound the stage, and anyone who is nearby, and myself.

We will strip the music of pretension and complexity, and it will be like having sex with Nosirrah, very, very short, in length—and in time. And confusing. But powerful, maybe even mystical. And then you want to throw up, at least that is what the last few women did when they sobered up and got a look at me. That is why I always suggest keeping the lights off when having an intimate encounter with Nosirrah, and just as a back up, wearing a blindfold, and usually, earplugs because I do a lot of high pitched screaming in those brief moments of ecstasy, oh, and a nose plug, because I don't have access to running water except at the bathroom in the gas station down the street and then I can only do my pits real quick because that pink liquid soap stings my sores and maybe it would be good to wear a wetsuit or something like that just to avoid skin to skin contact as much as possible. But these women who came to Nosirrah were brave, and at $20 a date I would expect no less, but they still lost their dinner when they gazed at me. In truth, it sometimes happens to me, too, when I look in the mirror, but I try not to do that right after eating.

Puke Rock is a fitting name, but maybe I should name it after the punks who are going to be part of it, maybe something direct and to the point, straight from the street punks, catchy like Angry Youth Rock. I will go faster with the guitars, heavier with the drums, we will go as fast as possible, then faster, and we will see what catches fire.

The original punk and puke was Diogenes the Cynic, a sour fellow in ancient Greece who just wouldn't submit to social norms, and if they had invented guitars back then, I am sure he would have been on stage playing fast. As it was, he lived in the streets in the public market place and lived like a dog, a species, by the way, he idolized for the dog's total freedom of expression. He urinated, defecated and masturbated and no doubt puked in public as proof that truth and happiness lay in the freedom from convention, not adherence to it. In short, he was honest, and more importantly, he made the point of how dishonest society was in its pretensions. His only regret upon masturbating in the city center was that he couldn't similarly relieve himself of hunger by rubbing his belly. Diogenes is Nosirrah's patron saint, and I believe that I must be related to him, no, let me speak the truth just as Diogenes would have it, for I am without care or attachment to the world of things or rules, in truth, I am Diogenes reincarnate.

There you have it, and you no doubt think I am mad, but like it or not, I am Diogenes the Dog reborn to bring the truth without compromise to this planet once more. You want proof, of course. Bits and pieces of my past in ancient

Greece have leaked through into this incarnation, for example I spontaneously understand words in Greek although I have never studied it even for a day: eureka, feta, falafel, Zorba, the list goes on but I won't bore you who cannot speak even one word of this language from the cradle of western civilization. How could I know these words if I were not a reborn Greek, you think I'm meshugennah, ah, but that word is probably Greek to you, too.

There is more, I have faint memories in which I am with Antisthenes, my teacher, the real founder of the school of Cynics. He wasn't The Man, but he was the student of The Man, and you know who that is, of course, Socrates was The Man, Antisthenes was his protégé, and Nosirrah nee Diogenes was the disciple of Antisthenes. This is what I learned from Antisthenes: all of what we talk about, all of what we worry about, all of what we are in conflict about, are abstractions of the mind that do not exist outside of our references. Antisthenes, I called him Anti, was not into definitions, generalizations, concepts, he considered these as unreal. Something is what it is and when you describe it, that description is not the it, the description is an abstraction from the it or a repetition of the it, so why bother with adjectives, adverbs or other unnecessary embellishments. The world is present without the requirement of descriptors. Anti wasn't a great conversationalist, imagine:

"Anti, how are you doing today?"

"I am."

"Well, Anti, at least it is a beautiful day here in sunny ancient Greece where western civilization is being cradled and olives are being grown."

"It is day."

"Anti, I have been having a lot of questions about the nature of life."

"Nosirrah, also known as Diogenes, I cannot see your questions, or this life you mention, I can only observe you making sounds."

"Anti, if you keep this up Plato is going to steal your thunder, he's going to plagiarize Socrates, take your best riffs, and with his marketing, he is going to end up being The Man now that Socrates got hemlocked."

"Nosirrah, Plato is an asshole. And you see, this is just repeating a fact not elucidating it. Plato and asshole are the same, just repeating what is, as if we have understood it better."

"What shall I do, then?"

"Seek not pleasure, but live in the virtue of truth."

"But, Anti, truth means expressing without restraint. I have to pee right now, shall I go right here in the marketplace?"

"Nosirrah, better insanity than the conditioning of pleasure and the slavery to public approval. Be what you are, that is all that you can be. There is nothing else."

And so I relieved myself at that moment of enlightenment of the burden of my self image, and, as well, my full bladder much to the horror of those passing by, and, indeed, I got it all over Anti's new sandals and toga so he never talked to me again which was no big change in our relationship. He had given me the gift of deconstruction, the gift of anti from Anti. Nosirrah or Diogenes, by whatever name, is what he is, no more or less, and I took my lantern and began looking for another who was truthful to engage with. Now, in another lifetime, I am still looking for one who is honest without reserve, maybe it is you who reads these words? If so, let us meet and piss on each other's shoes.

That lantern took me into another time and

*I am still looking for one who is
honest without reserve.*

place, in Germany, in the early 1800's, in Braun-
schweig, that is, and I am still Nosirrah, I am
still Diogenes, but I am now Bonaventura the
night watchman, walking the streets with my
lantern and staff, peering into the windows of
the townsfolk. I am looking for truth, but all I
get is a large helping of clergy, hypocrisy and
braunschweiger. Times have changed from the
era of the Greeks. The Devil has arrived in man's
mind, or is it that the Devil has made man's
mind? I see the Devil at work everywhere I look,
especially in the church establishment. At least
the Greeks had Diogenes, but who will these
Germans have to confront their conventions,
their belief in their culture that will lead them
to a dead end and destruction? They are making a deal with the Devil. I will have to mention this to Goethe when I see him if he isn't
too busy writing that play about some Doctor
Fist or Fast or something—what a waste of time,
who cares about doctors, they make too much
money mostly on the placebo effect which they
don't understand anyway.

And maybe it is just my lack of personal
hygiene or some of my somewhat grotesque
physical anomalies, but does your doctor seem

to want to rush through your exams, my doctors always seem to be on their way to someone else and just by chance stop in to see me, and then they seem to do everything but look. Once I was so angry at my doctor, I went in to his office and said to his receptionist, "Tell the doctor that The Invisible Man is here for an appointment." She came back and said, "He can't see you."

But that is not the worst of not being seen, once I went to the mountains to meditate, fast, and pray, hoping to lose myself in the divine worship of God. A fast moving storm came, and wouldn't you know it I was struck by lightning. Now I was fuming, literally, but I rolled around on the ground and put out the fire in my pants, but I mean to say I was mad, and screamed at God, "After all my spiritual work and worship on this mountain how can you send a lightning bolt!" An apologetic voice boomed out of the clouds, "Sorry, I didn't recognize you." That was just my imagination, or maybe not, maybe it was God's apology, or maybe I was never on the mountain and maybe that is another of Nebirk's jokes, but it isn't very funny when you are not seen by God or not seen by your doctor,

*After all my spiritual work, how can God send a lightning bolt!*

but that is redundant isn't it? If I dissolve myself in mystic realization, how would God recognize me?

That is the paradox. I have placed myself in my entirety, in my honesty, in the public square, in lifetime after lifetime, showing every bit of me, exposing myself, and all I have gotten has been some screams of revulsion, the occasional disorderly conduct arrest, and at least one marriage proposal from a bag lady with a nice all-chrome shopping cart which was pretty tempting, but never in all these times, places and incarnations has Nosirrah been truly seen by man or God. No man can see me, only their own mind is visible. God cannot see me, for the same reason, only God's mind is visible and in that mind God and I are not different. There is no Nosirrah, Nosirrah is not. Only Nosirrah believes that he is, and this belief is what he is. That's the paradox of One.

Nossirah's belief in God is also his belief in himself as the believer in God and so he is divided from One. They don't teach this kind of mathematics in schools, what is two divided from one? The answer is not in the school books, it is in the life that we live, and the answer is simple. If you divide two from one you have a schism that will leave you struggling for all of existence, like asking the question what is the value of pi.

The scientist and mathematicians have perked up, slide rules are being made ready, computer punch cards are being punched with Fortran efficiency, throats are being cleared with hands raised even as the calculations are being done.

I have suddenly become a high school mathematics teacher looking out onto the faces of eager and attentive students.

"Mr. Nosirrah, Mr. Nosirrah..."

"Yes, Edward, do you have the answer? Class pay attention, Edward is going to share his answer with us. Edward, what is the value of pi?"

"Mr. Nosirrah, the value of pi in its full decimal extension is: 3.14159265358979323846264 3383279502884197169399375105820974944592 3078164062862089986280348253421170679821 4808651328230664709384460955058223172535 9408128481117450284102701938521105559644 6229489549303819644288109756659334461284 7564823378678316527120190914564856692

234603486104543266482133936072602491412
737245870066063155881748815209209628292540917153643678925903600113305305488204665213841469519415116609..."

Now I am going to cut away from Edward's fine answer mainly because pi is a number that will never end and will never repeat itself. Edward will grow old giving this answer, he will never taste the moist lips of his first adolescent kiss, he will never get his first job, marry, have children, develop stress related psychological issues requiring increasing levels of psychotropic drugs so he can continue to produce income while his children ignore him other than whining about their lack of more and more things, and his wife becomes bloated beyond normal human dimensions by eating in front of the television pretty much all day and most of the night and his dog becomes indolent and incontinent, not even bothering to greet him at the door when he comes home and it is hardly noticed when he keels over with a heart attack other than to call the insurance agent to make sure that the life insurance policy will cover all of the ongoing expenses, and whatever the minimal burial expenses are these days, probably cremation and scattering since that saves on buying a plot and there is a special on cremation this month.

"...4330572703657595919530921861173819 3261179310511854807446237996274956735 1885 7527248912279381830119491298336733624406 5664308602139494639522473719070217986094 3702770539217176293176752384674818467669 4 0513200056812714526356082778577134275778 9609173637178721468440901224953430146549 5853710507922796892589235..."

Yes, while Edward is giving the answer to the value of pi, his entire life will go by and he will not have a life other than giving the answer, and he will die still giving the answer, and even if he were to reincarnate or simply become a ghostly apparition still standing in Mr. Nosirrah's 10th grade math class and giving the answer while all of time passes, the sun burns out, the solar system collapses, the universe falls into itself and then into a packed spot of totally condensed matter, energy and gravity in which there is nothing, not even nothing from nothing, still at this end of all time and space, Edward would still be giving his answer.

"...4201995611212902196086403441815981 3 6297747713099605187072113499999983729780

49951059731732816096318595024459455346908302642522230825334468503526193118817101000313783875288658753320838142061717766914730359825349042875546873115956286388235378759375195778185778053217122680661300192787661111959092164201989..."

The value of pi does not end. And it is the same if you seek God, if you divide two from one, there is no end to that search. When the universe has run out of time, and all that is known and all that is unknown collapses, and all matter has condensed into nothingness, Edward will still be calculating pi, and you will still be looking for God.

Edward cannot stop calculating even though his life, and all lives, are passing him by. Can you stop looking for God? Can you stop looking for the answer? Can you stop looking? Can you stop? Can you? You?

Edward, thank you, you can stop and sit down. Or would we rather Edward keep going, at least he is doing something. We have a deep respect for doing, doing is a kinetic narrative that gives us so much solace in an otherwise chaotic and pointless universe. In my case when I went off for years of meditation people said,

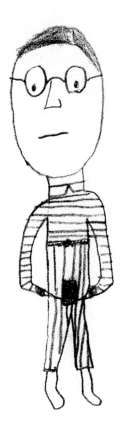

*Edward cannot stop
calculating even though
his life is passing him by.*

"At least then Nosirrah won't be sitting around doing nothing."

# 2

* * * * *

*I believe in general in a dualism between facts
and the ideas of those facts in human heads.*
                                    —GEORGE SANTAYANA

> *This couldn't be a dream
> For too real it all seems
> But it was just my imagination
> Once again
> Running away with me
> Tell you, it was just
> my imagination
> Running away with me*
>                                    —THE TEMPTATIONS

I FELL INTO A DEEP DUALITY.

Nosirrah's brain builds a world out of what
it knows and that can be a problem when you
are Nosirrah for I do not suffer from *le délire
de negation,* no, indeed I enjoy it. Jules Cotard
with his so-named Cotard's syndrome cannot understand this, nor Proust for that matter
with his *Remembrances of Things Past.* Cotard
thought it was a problem for a man to believe
that he himself did not exist, and worked in
asylums with those who insisted that they were
not there. Proust just muddied the waters with
his involuntary memories suggesting an out of
control mental world and therefore a persona
without reliable structure.

I am all of that and more, and it is all moving at such speed that one cannot say that I am
at all. Nosirrah's syndrome is like the bad seed
of Cotard's syndrome with involuntary memories. I have voluntary memories of being no one,
and involuntary memories of being no one, and
when I am free of memory of any kind I am
Nosirrah, and when I am free of being Nosirrah I am you and everything. Nothing, me,
you, everything, as you can see there are too

many objects in this world of duality, too much complexity and all of it from the occurrence of mind.

Perhaps I will bore you with the following account of more doctors trying to help me with electricity as their healing modality. But where Skinner failed, others tried. If you are bored by my repetitiveness then maybe these doctors can help you not feel so bored. Being plugged into electrical current is never boring. You will find your true self in the buzzing of the transformer and sizzle of melting synaptic connections that is heard within your mind and nowhere else. You will feel the immense creative flow as you express in shrieks and groans that have never before passed your lips.

I know that I am nobody, but my mind continues to construct a world with Nosirrah at the center. Even when the psychiatrists have given me the electroshocks, screaming at me in their maniacal glee, again and again, "Who feels this pain if there is no Nosirrah?" and I calmly mumble back, "Exactly, if you can exert such pain on a man and he still says he does not exist then this is just proof that he is right. But, worse for you dear doctors, you cannot ever show that

*Who feels this pain if there is no Nosirrah?*

you are right." Of course, they cannot prove that Nosirrah is, even as they demand proof from me that Nosirrah is not. They know that they have an indefensible position and this enrages them further. More voltage, larger injections, tighter restraints, but none of it can appease their fear and rage, fear that they do not exist either and rage that I remind them of that. For Nosirrah it is the irritation of trying to talk with a rubber block jammed in the mouth, like when the dentist loads up your mouth with rubber dams, cotton balls and instruments and then asks how your life is going.

My mind constructs these doctors of the psyche, my mind, like a castaway on an island left too long, gone mad, with only a friend made of coconut shells and palm fronds to talk to. For me it is the other whom I have imagined, so that I can exist. Without the other I am not and there is nothing. With the other I am still not, but there is something. It is the convoluted mind of Nosirrah that creates the other as beings who try to convince Nosirrah that he is when he knows that he is not, that they are not and that even his mind and all of its duality is not, even the convulsing electricity and the ensuing blankness is not.

Mind projects, it does not reflect, it creates the world it does not apprehend it. The mind that smiles sees a happy world and all the reasons for it, the mind that is in sorrow sees only tragedy. No mind sees no world. Nosirrah is perceptually impaired and sees from the world where he sees Nosirrah seeing the world. Nosirrah sees from the world not at the world. This is dualism in reverse and upside down and inside out, one plus one that equals two, or one or three. No rules, no logic, nothing fixed.

So you can shock me as you like, and I will sign any statement you like. I will confess to all the unsolved crimes, to being a communist sympathizer and to being a member in good standing of the Rotary Club. I will agree that I suffer from Cotard's syndrome and must take my pills and I will agree that I am enlightened and experiencing the great liberation. I will agree that I am Nosirrah, and I will agree that I am you. It makes no difference when I am not, when I am, when I am and am not.

Sheila sent me to those shock happy psychiatrists, not that I was showing any obvious symptoms of depersonalization other than not responding to Sheila's controlling demands, one of which was to be her boyfriend. We met at a funeral, she was there for a relative I suppose, I was there only relatively, but as a day laborer handling the spadework. One thing led to another and that another led to yet another, but that was in the realm of causality and would make a great story and certainly a far better novella than the one you are currently reading. Nothing led to this, in fact, because Sheila was from a dimension without causality, a place where her wants and needs were the defining terms of reality. She wanted me. Not just in a carnal way, but more like you wanted a hamster when you were in 3$^{rd}$ grade, unless that was a carnal hamster you desired in 3$^{rd}$ grade. Sheila wanted me, not a hamster, but she did want a pet. Maybe it was the tattoo that was so evident on my biceps bulging through the stained tank-top I was sweating in as I trowelled dirt on top of Uncle Bob or Aunt Betty, the tattoo that said *"Amor ordinem nescit"* which you will recognize from your seminary classes on the early centuries saints, but if you didn't attend seminary, are not Catholic or never heard of Saint Jerome, maybe you took Latin in high school. But in case you were not paying attention in Latin class, it means *Love does not know order.* What it means is really in the eye of the beholder or perhaps we should say in the interpretive brain of the projector. This phrase could mean that transcendental love is beyond form, or perhaps that love is just plain messy.

The story of how I got that tattoo might illustrate my understanding of this phrase, but let's just say that whatever my perspective was, it was entirely unconscious at the time of the tattooing through a combination of very inexpensive tequila, extreme tantric breath practices designed to extend and expand the pleasures of the body a thousandfold and a lovely senorita named Chitlalmina who if she was two or three decades younger, with some dental reconstruction and extreme weight loss would be considered modestly attractive in fairly dim light.

But there was love that knew no order for that one hour, although Chitlal seemed more interested in the professional wrestling on the television which she was somehow able to view by way of the mirrored ceiling—now that's tantra!

My little Chicolet, wherever you are, mi

amor, nunca me olvidaré de nuestra hora junto. Estoy apesadumbrado que no pagué sino que no tenía ningún dinero. And I forgive you for being angry with me when I could not pay, and your brother for his rather crude attempt at restitution with his defacing tattoo job (I didn't know he went to seminary—was that before or after his prison stretch?) and no, I didn't get hepatitis even though he kept spitting on the needles. I have contemplated the message on the tattoo all these years since Juarez, and the truth of these words, that love is bound by no law, just goes deeper and deeper, and I realized that you brought me that truth and that I will pay you the 400 pesos I owe you for that miraculous time. Contact my editor, she will make sure you get paid, but for God's sake tell her that it is for research you helped me with for my book *Chronic Eros* but don't go into too much detail, just research into Saint Jerome and the meaning of love without rules. One question for you my little Chitlalminitta, why did your brother choose to put this phrase under a picture of a pig? I have wracked my always overactive brain and cannot find the connection, our encounter of ultimate beauty and sensuality albeit in a rather déclassé room with hourly checkout, and I in the apex of my manhood although perhaps grossly emaciated at the time due to a series of bile cleansing fasts I had undergone in my quest for spiritual perfection that included limiting my food intake to lemon juice, cayenne pepper, olive oil, distilled water and pizza.

But I have been interrupted in my tale by my editor who with her awful red pencil has scrawled "repetitive, meandering and unfocused" along with "no one cares about your low-life women" and I have to agree with her, although she must be referring to my readers not caring, it is true that no one cares for Nosirrah's women the way he cares for them and while this makes my editor insanely jealous, and here comes the red pencil, all right Lydia, you are not insanely jealous, you are clear-eyed in your understanding of the weakness for women that is Nosirrah and which is his worship of the Divine Feminine Principle, now put down the red pencil so I can finish.

As I was saying, Sheila, though she may have been a dominatrix at heart, had something both perverse and profound to give me and it was not just the combination of using

her electric cattle prod and her double jointed
thumbs. Good heavens, the red pencil again,
Lydia, you must let me write, you cannot stop
me every sentence. I know that I went into all
of this in *Chronic Eros* and my sensual experi-
mentations are more suited for such a book,
and not a book about nothing. All right, all
right, Lydia, stop already, people are reading
here, please don't humiliate me in front of my
audience. Dear reader, you must obtain a copy
of *Chronic Eros* where you will find a full ac-
counting of Sheila and her initiation of me past
the outer form into the inner sanctum of eros
and thanatos, then deeper, thrusting into the
sanctum sanctorum of totem and taboo, and
then deeper still, into the garbhagriha where the
elemental forces of Shiva and Shakti meld into
one. This is the alchemy of two from nothing,
One from two, One into nothing.

Mercury, unstable, fragmenting, each glob-
ule easily broken into a dozen more identical
blobs of poisonous quicksilver mirroring the
world that it cannot fathom. This is the first
metal, the primary metal for the alchemist, out
of which all other metals are made. This is the
Mind, Mercury is Mind.

Mercury cannot bear the heat, the friction, the grinding of life itself, the mortar and pestle of the alchemist with a dash of brimstone, sulfur the fire element of transformation. Mind undergoes a transmutation. Mercury becomes gold, what was unstable becomes stable. The mystery of alchemy produces gold, pure, shining, immutable, stable consciousness.

Gold from mercury and sulphur. Pure consciousness from mind transformed in the fire of life. The Mind that once moved with any stimulus now holds still in the face of all things. Everything has become nothing and what faces that everything has become nothing. Nothing from nothing.

∞

* * * * *

*Our knowledge can only be finite, while our ignorance must necessarily be infinite.*

—KARL POPPER

*Two things are infinite: the universe and human stupidity; and I'm not sure about the the universe.*

—ALBERT EINSTEIN

I FELL INTO AN ENDLESSLY DEEP HOLY.

One thing, two things, no things, all things, infinite things. Is the universe out there? Is it a place of objects that the mind identifies, describes and understands? Is the universe an interior experience without any correlation, yet an experience that suggests an objective correlation simply for its own sanity? Is there nothing at all, not even the evanescent wisps of mind? Is there everything, infinite universes of all possibility, co-existing yet hardly in communion with each other?

Nosirrah was given the task to unravel these mysteries of sense and reality and he was given only one tool of all possible tools and that is the perception that flows through him unbidden, unregulated and unstable. I once considered it my task to become fully aware of this perception and that this awareness would be the key to the understanding, but chasing awareness is like chasing your tail, not that it is an unending pursuit, which it is, but we don't have a tail to chase, and we don't have awareness to chase either.

I am aware or I am not aware. If I am aware then I am and if I am not aware then there is nothing at all. This understanding came on its own, and not through my pursuit of awareness. This understanding destroyed my life, with its hopes and dreams, leaving me as I am and nothing more, nothing less.

Yet, still there is the question of the whole, the divided, the nothing and the everything.

Mahavira said it was all a relative world in which the endless viewpoints described, but could never know, the whole. We all know the story of the blind men and the elephant in which each described the part that he could touch, the man who grabbed the trunk described a pipe, the man who touched the ears a fan, the one who felt the leg a tree, the one the torso a drum. Each could describe a part, none could describe the whole.

When a nice Jain was telling this to me once during my wanderings through India, I thought he had missed the real meaning of the story. It wasn't just that the blind men were only perceiving the parts, what about the elephant? Look at it from the elephant's perspective, all of a sudden a bunch of blind guys start groping you, that must be really freaky, so maybe you just stomp on all of them repeatedly until they stop groping or stop breathing which ever comes first. Then maybe you do some trumpeting just to let off steam and eat some leaves or peanuts or something to relax. That's the whole point of the story, you just have to relax in the end because it is all pretty complicated so why stress. Of course they shoot the elephant because you have to do that to a rogue elephant, especially if he stomps on a bunch of blind guys even if they were grabbing where they shouldn't be. The End. At least that is the way I heard the story when I was a child, but I think the baby sitter was possibly drunk or deranged or both.

I am sure that Mahavira explained all of this elephant and blind guys deep meaning in 600 BC when he was doing his preaching but they didn't write his material down for a thousand years so you can imagine that a lot of good stuff got lost. The Jain guy who was talking to me in India became a little unsettled about my interpretation, and seemed to be hyperventilating and even though I kept shouting at him to relax and take off the damned surgical mask so he could breathe better, he just got up and ran away, probably stepping on ants and spiders the whole way. So much for ahimsa.

Perhaps the symbolism of the story is more obvious to you who are reading this richly layered book and constructing deep meaning from

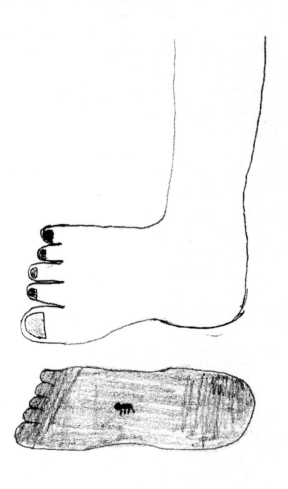

*So much for ahimsa.*

it. It is all there: the whole, the divided, the nothing and the everything. Every category of division and non-division, subject and object, dual and non-dual subsumes into nothing.

When I faced nothing I didn't leave the structures of normal concept so much as that my concepts were engulfed in something else. Nothing is everything that has been discarded to get to what I know. Seeing the unlimited nature of what I had given up to know something, I came to see that I knew nothing. Nothing began to speak to me more and more as what I knew receded into its own self-made obsolescence. I was in space without a suit, and I exploded, silently, into infinite nothings.

Is this the movement of nothing into something, as we cycle through birth, as we live in dream and transcendental experience, as we touch into the enlightenment of unity, and ultimately death and transmigration? If we have a guide to take us through the various antarabh va, perhaps a *Book of the Dead*-toting lama, then we believe we might manage. But I am sorry to report that Nosirrah cannot be helped by the Tibetans any more than he can help them with the Chinese. Nosirrah is not

Tibetan, just like the Tibetans are not Chinese.

Nosirrah's bardo is non-navigable, there is no rebirth as there was no birth prior, the bardo is the incarnation and the incarnation is the bardo. I have flowed through the six bardos and the six hell realms as a deva, an asura, an animal, a hungry ghost, a human being and a hell being. I have visited the ten spiritual realms, do you know these from your Buddhist studies? They range from Hell realms to realms of joy, and in the end there is Buddhahood.

Nosirrah became a Buddha, and I followed the final precepts of my vows, "As a bodhisattva I shall strive for as long as illusion endures to liberate all sentient beings and therefore to deliver them to Nirvana. I do not seek Awakening for myself but for all other beings which I shall do by cultivating supreme moral perfection and collect uncountable amounts of merit which will be dedicated to all other sentient beings. And finally, if I meet the Buddha on the road I will kill him!"

Nosirrah killed the Buddha there and then, metaphorically speaking, that is to say that Nosirrah killed Bodhisattva Nosirrah thereby failing miserably at my vows to achieve moral perfection, collect uncountable amounts of merit or deliver anyone to Nirvana. I was the perfect Buddha and was not the perfect Buddha. I knew then that all that I had done, all that I had understood, all that I had accumulated and expressed, including every realm, every incarnation, every Buddhahood was nothing at all and had never been anything, only everything.

The universe is happening all around the tiny world circumscribed by what I know and in the face of the relentless intensity of what I do not know I leave the small but grandiose Nosirrah forever. I find I cannot use the beyond to leave my little self, for it is using me. I am the slave of the energy beyond this little creature whose brain continues to pump out stories of how the universe is, yet it is the universe that pumps those stories in so that Nosirrah can pump them out. I see what I am looking for because, of course, Noisirrah's mind is constructing what it is seeing.

Our finest ability is to miss practically everything that is going on, isn't that a cosmic joke, all you seekers of enlightenment, that our greatest ability is to not be aware. I don't have the capacity to see, hear, feel, smell everything, so

I perceive only what I focus on. I don't perceive almost everything. What I focus on is what I want, what I need, what allows me to survive, what I desire. A gorilla could walk through the room and I might miss it if I was focused on a beautiful woman, but a beautiful woman could not walk through the room and be missed by Nosirrah. I see what is important to me, and there is absolutely nothing in life that is more interesting than a beautiful woman, except two beautiful women, of course.

Someday, the psychologists will show that this is just the way the brain is built, not just my brain, but unfortunately for you, your brain too. You construct, you call it reality and you create your narrative to keep it all intact. Even now you are doing this, in this sentence, and will you find meaning in the fact that a gourd has blown across the ocean where penguins dance hurriedly amongst voters angry at the lack of yoghurt? This is gibberish, no it is art, no its modernism and anti-art, it is my childhood, my future, it is nothing important, but it is always something, don't you make something of it, and of this?

It is good that the mind works in this way,

as it will allow me to skip to an entirely different subject matter without any kind of reason-
able bridging material which might suggest that
I have not the faintest capacity as a writer, or
that I have some kind of thought disorder, but
you will not notice this non sequitur because
you will be busy making connections from the
last paragraph to the next paragraph, connections that exist only in the confines of your own
mind. But in a strange twist of synchronicity it
is those very confines of the mind that intro-
duce us to the next paragraph, and indeed the
subject of what happens when those limitations
are unleashed.

While you may not immediately see the
connection between a leash and a vaccination,
watch carefully as you make the connection and
note that it is your mind not just the symbols
on this page that are creating the remarkable
link, although I must congratulate myself on the
clever use of "unleashed" as both a metaphor
for total freedom from the known and the con-
crete description of a strap by which an animal
is restrained or let go. I was fortunate to be
vaccinated at an early age, and this, you must
remember, was before vaccination was cool. I

don't mean the regular shots that a child gets for smallpox or the sugar cube for polio. I had some trouble in my youth with a compulsion to bite, and due to the size and sharpness of my teeth this became an issue in my neighborhood where people, in my opinion, were a bit over-protective of their dogs. For whatever reason, I enjoyed the sense of accomplishment and mastery when I had the neck of a German Shepherd firmly clenched in my mouth, jaw squeezing ever so tight, or running after a panicked collie and catching it just at its heel with my front teeth. I didn't have many friends, well none except Nebirk, so it is no wonder I took to chasing down dogs, and I never ate them, and mostly left them with flesh wounds but nothing more dramatic than that. So I was reported to the dog catcher, who reported me to the American Society for the Prevention of Cruelty to Animals, who at first wanted to neuter me, but in the end just vaccinated me for rabies and distemper and ordered my guardians to keep me on a leash at all times.

Now, many people are against vaccinations and make the case that these injections poison the body, ruin the health and the minds of

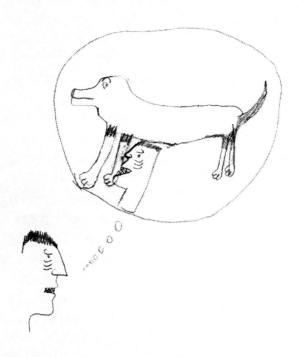

*I had some trouble in my youth
with a compulsion to bite.*

young children. Some dare suggest that disease rates go up in areas that are vaccinated and that diseases disappear on their own in a population or due to advances in hygiene and water treatment. Some foolish ignoramuses even suggest that we should spend our efforts on exercise, proper nutrition and stress reduction so as to boost our natural immune system to all disease. To those, and all others who would question the efficacy of vaccinations, I say, "Grrrrr, woof, woof." I am sorry that slipped out. Ever since my rabies and distemper shots I find myself at times growling and barking, and sometimes chasing my tail, come to think of it that tail started growing around the time of those shots. But, I have to defend those vaccinations because I have never ever had rabies or distemper, and I wonder how many of you critics can say that? These shots are perfectly safe, except for those few exceptions for whom they are perfectly unsafe. So don't think of vaccinations as medicine, think of them as lottery tickets, and hope that you are lucky.

I would say that besides a little side effect of barking and a tail-like protrusion coming from the base of my spine, the main benefit of my vaccinations was the way it altered my brain. Yes, as I have recounted in my semi-autobiographical novella *Practical Obsession*, I did have the early near-birth experience of death and that was transformative, leaving me trying to piece together a coherent reality for much of my childhood. But it was my vaccinations that turned the cabbage of my brain into coleslaw, creating a side-dish of my personality that would never again be a main course. What then would be the entrée, if not the "me"? From what do you live if your cabbage is in shreds? The answer of course should have been obvious, but it was only after years of reintegration, the attempt to put Humpty back together again, to find the rebirthing primal scream gestalt do-your-thing-I'll-do-mine, drop-out-tune-in-turn-on high that would unshred the cabbage, but I may have lost the train of my ever speeding thought here, so I will change the subject once again.

But before I do that, I should mention that there was one side effect of my vaccination that you might find of interest which is that I developed prosopagnosia which is a disorder of face perception where you don't recognize faces, human faces that is, I could tell dog from dog easily enough but all humans looked pretty much the same and while I'm pretty certain I had this condition I couldn't be absolutely certain because I couldn't tell if it was me since I couldn't recognize my own face either, suggesting the possibility that it was someone else who could not recognize my face, but of course it was equally likely that it was someone else who could not recognize their own face. It also crossed my mind that everyone had been replaced with imposter look-alikes and I couldn't recognize them because they were actually someone else. Someday I would like to examine this question with a good psychiatrist but so far I have only found imposter psychiatrists and they can be quite dangerous, don't you think?

But, the real issue with faces is really how do we know who we are? Why do we think that is our face in the mirror? When I look in the mirror, after the waves of nausea pass, I see a stranger, an unknown being, a mystery. I ask myself questions like, if I comb my hair with my right hand, the mirror man is combing with his left hand, then how is it he is not standing on his head? Try it and you will see what I mean. Isn't that evidence enough that this entity I call

*Why do we think that is our face in the mirror?*

me isn't actual? I can't really ever see me, but I assume I am there. I look in the mirror and assume that is me. I look at a photo and assume that is me. But I can never look directly at myself and believe me I have tried, which is why I am severely cross-eyed. There does not appear to be anyone who is looking, just various objects that I say is the looker, but isn't that just a guess, an assumption, an inference. What I can directly see is the whole scope of my sight and is this not what I am—what I see is what I am? Try it. See what you can see.

What I see is a world full of imposter people, poseurs who convince each other that they are their bodies, their words, their faces, their histories, but in truth each of these aspects are fiction, they are imposters making up the theater piece of their life and selling tickets for the drama to each other. None can admit that they know nothing in the least about the nature of the reality in which they swim, each moves quickly past that moment each morning when they glance in the mirror and are shocked that they do not recognize what looks back, so shocked that they quickly create the narrative that, of course, that is their face, and that face goes with a story, and that face and story need to go to work, or to school, or to war.

But if you look and don't flinch you will see through the eyes of the one looking back and from the mirror world, our world is one of undifferentiated, unrecognizable life without location, this is the original face that the Zen koan refers to, the face before the face, the face that we cannot admit that we have forgotten. We do not recognize our original face, so we do work-arounds, memory aids, substitutes for that recognition and we accept that the imposter face that stares back at us from the mirror is who we are, and that this is the face from which we look. Consider this: you have no direct proof of having a face at all, you only have the fiction of your own history and like all history it is the writer of that account who creates the past, and that past defines he who writes it.

Now, I will actually change the subject.

I was approached early in my career by those who are powerful and well placed in the publishing and literary world, but they really just represented one more powerful than all of them, to whom they were just slaves. I was offered stardom, I would be acclaimed, interviewed, my books studied in graduate schools and found in every bookstore around the world. I would have to make changes in my style, I would have to take out a few offensive phrases, but most of all I would have to attack hope, compassion and love as antiquated drivel unworthy of a modern pragmatic life. In short, I would have to help undermine all that was decent in the human being and bring out all that was the very worst. I would have fame and all that goes with it.

Please understand that this was all quite acceptable to me as I am a man without qualms, without moral ground, only guided by the ever expressing release of energy by the nothing that is everything, I know nothing at all about good and evil, well, not that I know nothing about it, just that I get the two confused so much that I never know which is which.

It was the Devil himself that offered me this fame, and I might have taken the bargain, but I was a bit wary having watched my share of *Twilight Zone*, and remembered well the tricks the horned one likes to play to gather the souls of men, but more than that, I wanted one thing more from the Devil in addition to fame and that was Julie Christie.

I am not so deluded to think that I was the only one who saw *Doctor Zhivago* and fell in love with Lara, but I felt like I was the only one who really understood her and that she was looking right at me and there was a special magic between us. I could tell Julie could hardly stand that Egyptian guy Omar Sharif they had cast her with and who would believe an Arab guy as a Russian anyway, maybe put him with Elizabeth Taylor in *Cleopatra*, or maybe David Lean should have made a sequel to *Lawrence of Arabia* and Omar could have starred in that since he did okay in the first one.

Julie—I think of her as Lara—wanted me, and I wanted her, and I was prepared to sell out the whole human race to have her, even to deal with the Devil himself. The Devil cursed, which is really something to hear. He did not control Julie, just as I suspected, she was too beautiful, intelligent and she did not care a wit about fame—she was beyond the Devil, and she wasn't even remotely religious, she was religion itself, in my opinion, of course. The cloven-hoofed one could not deliver Julie to me, and without Julie, nothing the Devil could offer me would work. He tried. He even offered a television show, *Nosirrah Tonight*. It was just a late night show on some obscure UHF channel, but I would be the star. He offered me the governorship of California, but I didn't want to live in Sacramento and I couldn't be president because there is some evidence that I was born in Berlin, and the Devil had already made a deal with Nixon anyway.

The Devil pulled out his final and most tempting offer, a book review in the *New York Times*, and I almost cracked. I knew that fame was my best hope for fulfilling my love for Julie Christie, for Lara Antipova, God just saying her name makes me break out in Russian passion, "Вы будете моей поистине влюбленностью, теперь и всегда. Я не insane, как раз сумашедше в влюбленности, о'кейе, возможно маленькое insane," which I will not translate for you, it is just for Lara. But even as I made my demand of the Devil, I also knew that just as in the movie, this love was not meant to be.

But let me ask you something, not to distract from my main thesis of extraordinary love for Julie Christie, but was that Lara at the end of the movie that Dr. Z saw from the streetcar, or was it just someone who reminded him of Lara, or was he suffering from clonal pluralization syndrome as I often do? This is really the raw depth and profundity of that film, does the Egyptian guy who is pretending to be a Russian pretend to die because he made a mistake and ran after the wrong beautiful, blond hottie from Wales who is pretending to be Russian, or the actual beautiful, blond hottie from Wales who is pretending to be Russian? Wouldn't that be a real tragedy if it was the wrong actress, maybe just an extra that was hired for the day, and all that method acting was squandered, or did they keep the footage anyway even though he was pretending to pine for the wrong actress?

I watched Dr Zhivago 316 times when it first came out, but that was mainly because I was homeless and that was what was showing at the all night theater on Market Street at the time, plus there was lots of leftover popcorn on the floor when I got hungry and the only other choice was the Mitchell Brothers on O'Farrell and that place had so many theme rooms and stages and females in various stages of undress that I never could get any sleep and then to get some sleep you just have to sit around the bus station nodding off all day, or sell blood at the Red Cross place and get a round trip ticket to anywhere four hours away to get your eight hours of beauty sleep. I much preferred sleeping with Julie Christie, and I learned Russian in my sleep on top of that just like in those sleep learning systems they are always trying to sell on TV, although my Russian is limited to the lines from the movie and I do have a heavy Egyptian accent. But I digress from the story of how the Devil tried to tempt me.

The Devil was offering me fame, without my beloved Lara? I looked the Devil in the eyes, all three of them, which is not that easy to do except, as I mentioned, being cross-eyed as I am gives me some advantage, and said he could take his fame and go straight to Hell, which in hindsight wasn't that much of a threat.

In the end raw fame really means nothing to Nosirrah. Nosirrah only shrinks deeper into the shadows as the spotlight searches for him. Nosirrah seeks not the fifteen minutes of fame, but fifteen minutes of sanity (in which I hope to write my greatest novella yet, *Fifteen Minutes of Sanity: Not a Novella Just a Run on Sentence*, where I will outline my vision for a new world order and reveal a new formula using all natural materials to clean shower mildew.

Maybe, instead of Hell, I should have told the Devil to go to Albrightsville, a strange enough name for a depressed town in the former coal mining region of Pennsylvania, where inbreeding has made the town name even a more hideous joke. It is not on the wrong side of the tracks, it is more or less directly on the tracks of the old coal trains taking off the black rock to Pittsburgh and Bethlehem, the trains are gone, the steel mills are gone, and the tracks are gone, leaving just the decaying cottages of the former miners. All that is left of that former glory is towards the mountains some miles, where the wealthy once went to play at the Grand Lady of the Poconos, the Inn at Pocono Manor, and where I, Nosirrah once lost a fortune to a Quaker card shark, a fortune not even mine, but the collective wealth of the good citizens of Albrightsville, not that they actually noticed, as the ability to add and subtract had been bred out of them generations before.

Yes, the Quakers built the Inn, bringing their Philadelphia wealth, and no, they are not supposed to play cards, but they have no priests to keep them in line and if the Devil came to them they would love him into submission. I should have sent the Devil to Albrightsville and had the Quakers deal with him, and yes, that pun was intended for I may have lost a fortune but I have never lost my ability to laugh. I do have trouble with stopping the laughing, but hitting my head against the wall sometimes helps.

But it was not just a fortune I lost to that Quaker, Jebediah Lippincott was his name, but my honor, my courage, my good name, yes, it was in Albrightsville that I was left with nothing, but this was nothing from something, mostly the Albrightsville Schools Fund, and also, as I recall the Parks Fund. I was Deputy Mayor at the time, and who knows, by now they will have named a street after me, but probably not a park. But I have told the tale of Albrightsville in my semi-autobiographical novella *Practical Obsession* and I will not repeat it here. Suffice it to say that I gambled on something from something, and got nothing from something.

Rarely have I gotten something for nothing, although I have tried many times. I have answered every offer mailed to me with great sincerity, every sweepstakes, free issue magazine offer and free life insurance, but none of these have given me anything but an endless stream of bills. I used to get so angry at the tricks played on me by these free offers, that I would take their postage paid envelope and tape it to a well packaged brick getting satisfaction from the notion that these mail-order cons would have to pay an onerous amount to simply find out what was inside. I had to stop when the outside wall in my apartment collapsed. I had no idea the bricks were anything structural, but I guess they were. I was behind in my rent anyway, so I moved on.

Then a few days later, I was picked up hitch-hiking through southern Utah by a rough and wizened fellow named Frank, quart bottle of Co-ors between his legs, mumbling about the wife who kicked him out, just looking for company but not looking who it was, not caring who it was, not that I could help him with a lifetime of hard living and bad drinking. He was only weaving a little, and there was no one else on those back roads, so I relaxed in the front seat and watched the desert go by. A radio show came in for a few seconds before fading out again, there isn't much in the way of reception out there, and it sounded like it was Charlton Heston, and somehow I imagined it was the voice of God and he was talking right to me, saying, "The religious confront the end of belief by embracing fundamentalism or ecumenicalism. The atheist reacts with strident unbeliever fundamentalism or the softer secular humanism. None seems to see that the other, the opposite, is the same. Madalyn Murray O'Hair and Bishop Fulton Sheen are believers, they believe that what they believe is what is true. Nothing is true. Believe in nothing. Not the nothing that is the opposite, but the nothing from nothing."

The radio station faded out as we drove out of range, and I didn't know if it was really God or not, but I saw clearly that I would one day write a book on the scourge of belief in all its forms, a book so powerful that the human race could move on to a new culture, not based on belief, but on what it is that lies beyond the human need to tell a story and the need to believe that story to feel safe. In this book I tell the story of nothing, so believe in nothing if you still crave the safety of a story. In the next book, I will take away even that belief, I will take away all belief, I will take away everything and more importantly I will take away nothing.

On that hot and dusty day, windows cranked down to pull in as much desert air as was possible in a Ford Fairlane, I saw that there were two seemingly insurmountable barriers to writing the next paradigm shattering book, a book of absolute transformation, and these two monumental obstructions were both beliefs. First, I believed that I was Nosirrah, that I existed. Second, I believed that God existed, an overriding intelligent and loving force for good. These beliefs would have to be obliterated to discover what lay beyond. Nosirrah's existence hung by a fragile thread, and this could fall away at any moment, but how would I ever destroy the belief in God unless God in his grace did the destruction? That was a contradiction, a paradox, an absurdity, an utter impossibility, and yet it must be.

I looked at Frank, his slurred rantings going on and on about his shambles of a life, cowboy shirt dotted with dribbles of chewing tobacco and ketchup from too many days without a change, his stubbly, leather-skin face scarred from hitting the floor in too many bars.

Then Frank looked at me for a moment, a

moment so intense and timeless that his brown bloodshot eyes cleared to pure piercing, bottomless blue and I looked through him to all of eternity and he looked at me with only love, nothing else, nothing but love, a pure conduit to some other dimension.

As I rode at breakneck speed over the hairpin turns, my vision was clear, God will reveal that which is beyond all knowing and all belief, and Nosirrah will write it, no matter the price that must be paid. God has created Nosirrah to discover what is beyond Nosirrah, and what is beyond God, of this there was certainty. Now this certainty would have to face the fear of uncertainty, the fear of unknowing, to go over the cliff to certain death, not as a metaphor but in reality, as it appeared I was now going over an actual cliff, along with Frank who had fallen into a drunken stupor and the Ford Fairlane in which I rode which caught fire as it tumbled bumper over bumper all the way down the steep canyon wall to the dark ravine of nothingness so far below the roadway that even the sound of the final cataclysmic impact was swallowed up in silence.